Anna Wilson

Jenny Løvlie

The Wide, Wide Sea

nosy

To Chloe and Lottie – A.W.

For my parents who let me roam freely,
and always answered all my questions – J.L.

First published in 2020 by Nosy Crow Ltd
The Crow's Nest, 14 Baden Place
Crosby Row, London, SE1 1YW
www.nosycrow.com

ISBN 978 1 78800 643 9 (HB) • ISBN 978 1 78800 704 7 (PB)
Nosy Crow and associated logos are trademarks
and/or registered trademarks of Nosy Crow Ltd

'The National Trust' and the oak leaf logo are registered trademarks of The National Trust (Enterprises)
Limited (a subsidiary of The National Trust for Places of Historic Interest
or Natural Beauty, Registered Charity Number 205846).

Text copyright © Anna Wilson 2020 • Illustrations copyright © Jenny Løvlie 2020
The right of Anna Wilson to be identified as the author and
Jenny Løvlie to be identified as the illustrator of this work has been asserted.

A CIP catalogue record for this book is available from the British Library.

Printed in China
Papers used by Nosy Crow are made from wood grown in sustainable forests.

1 3 5 7 9 8 6 4 2 (HB) • 1 3 5 7 9 8 6 4 2 (PB)

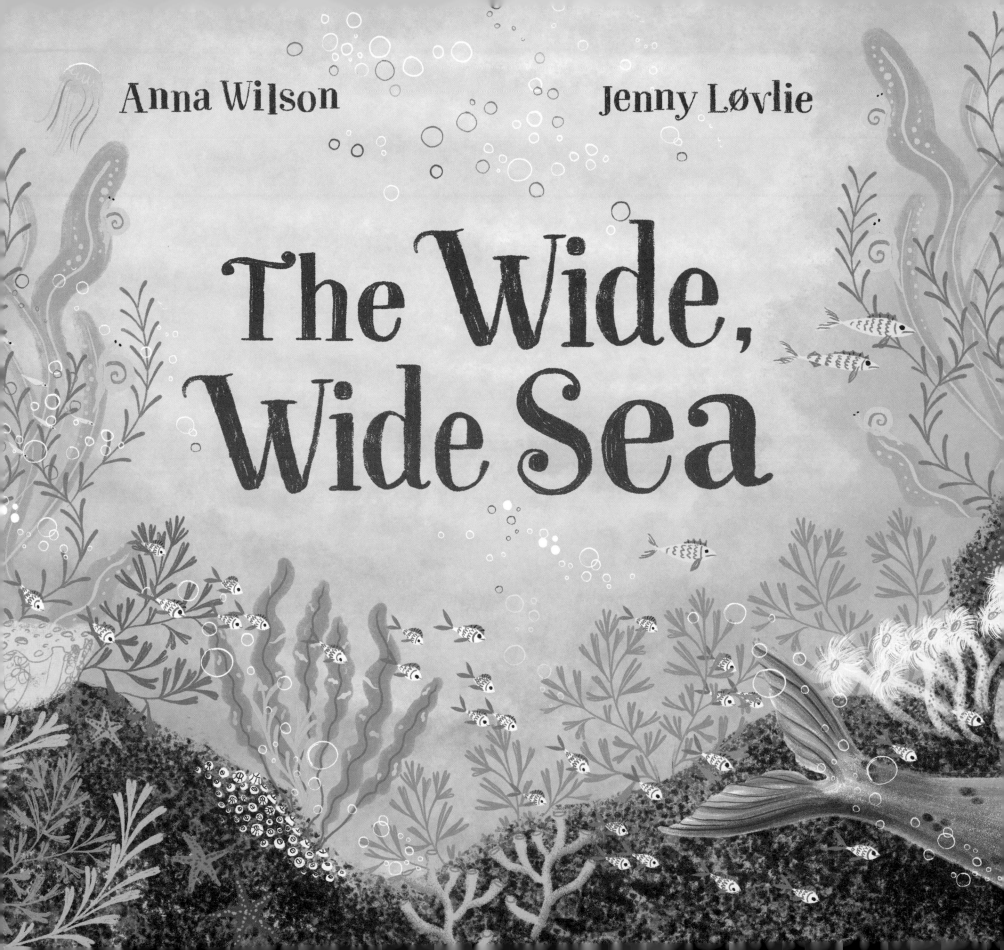

Anna Wilson   Jenny Løvlie

The Wide, Wide Sea

"This is the best place in the
Whole Wide World!" I shout.

"Slow down!" Gran laughs.

But I can't.

We pick up
pebbles,
driftwood,
shells.

I sit and count my seaside treasures.
Limpets, periwinkles, cuttlefish and whelks.

Gifts from the sea for me to keep.

"Look!" says Gran. "A seal!"

"Oh!" I shout, then stop.
I don't want to scare him.

"He's looking at me."
"Of course. You're on his beach."
"His beach?"
"Yes. It's his home."

I take a step towards the seal.
Into his home ...

into
the wide,
wide sea.

I wish I were a seal.

I would plunge through the glassy green ripples.

Down among the seaweed and the fishes.

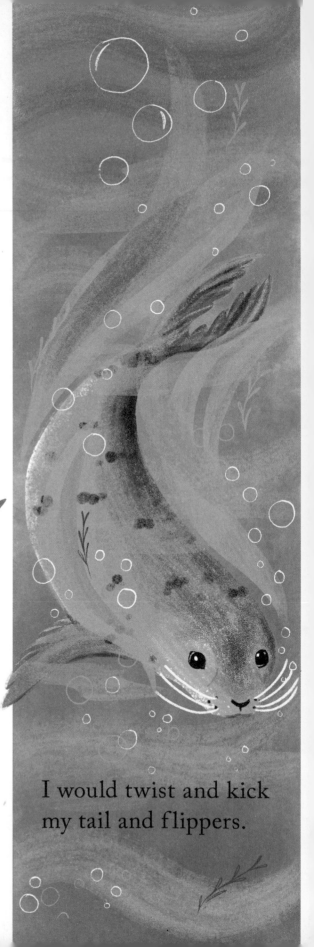

I would twist and kick my tail and flippers.

Swimming in an underwater
wonder world of

anemones
and crabs
and tiny snails.
Of shrimps
and starfish
and sea squirts.

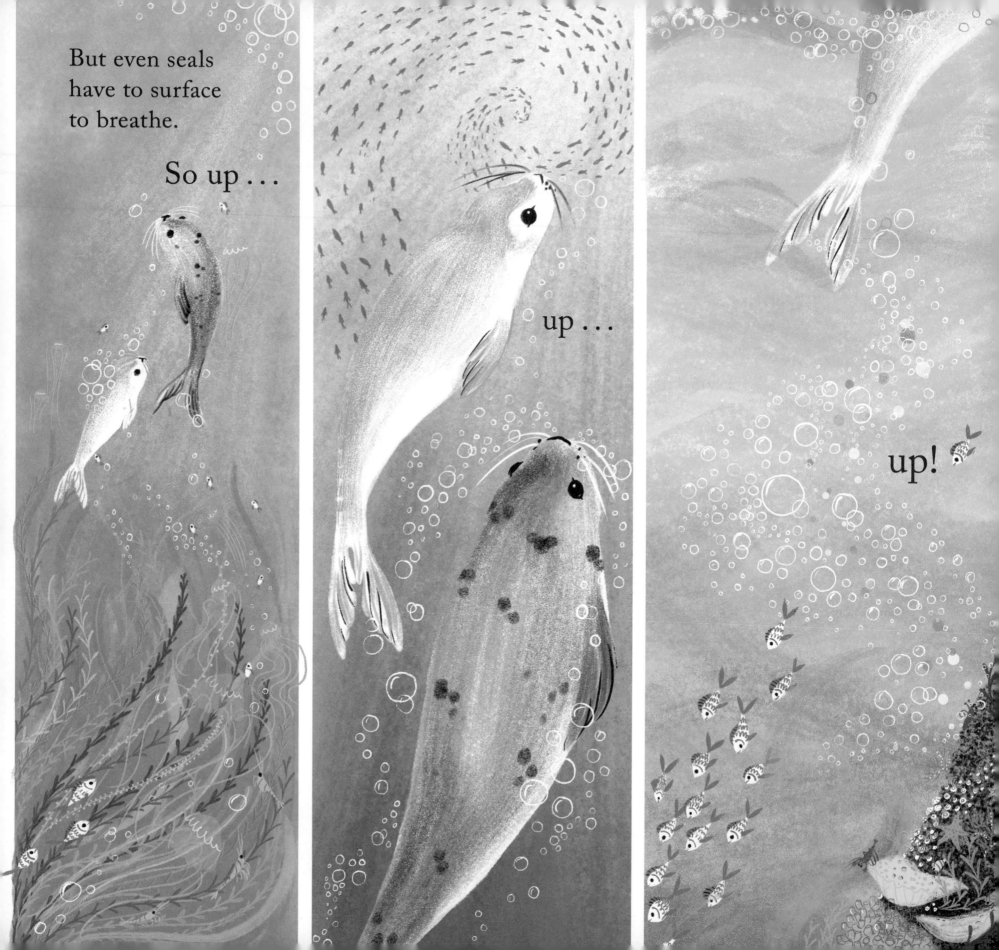

But even seals have to surface to breathe.

So up . . .

up . . .

up!

"My seal has gone! Where did he go?"
Gran snuggles me dry.
"He's gone to hunt for food," Gran says.
"He'll be back."

I sit and watch . . .

the gulls

and the sandpipers

and the gannets

and the kittiwakes.

I search the waves for my
seal's dark eyes.

But black clouds are rolling in.
"There's a storm brewing," Gran says.

"It's time for us to go home."

The sky cracks white with lightning spears.
"My seal . . . !"

"He'll dive deep, and keep safe," Gran says. "Let's get you off to bed."

The air rumbles and roars.

I toss and turn and dream.
My sheets are
giant sea-waves.

I dive and
see my seal.

We play...

and chase.

It's calm down here in
the deep dark water.

We're far away from
the storm's wild waves.

The pale sun ribbons
through the sea.
The storm has passed.

When I wake up, everything is different.

Wild.
Broken.
Messy.

"Will my seal be there? At his beach?"

"Let's see." Gran smiles.

Trees have fallen.
Branches, twigs and leaves lie like a lumpy carpet
on the narrow cliff path.

Yesterday the light danced.
The water glistened.
The towering rocks gleamed.

Today the sky is sulky dove-grey.
The air is quiet and frowning.

And the beach is full of things that shouldn't be here.
Salty tears sting my eyes. "Who did this?"

"We did." Gran smiles sadly. "People did."

"This isn't my mess!" I shout.

"I know," says Gran.
"But we can pick it up."

"This was the best place
in the Whole Wide World,"
I say. "Until today."

Then I hear shouts. Friendly greetings.
Gran waves to the people climbing,
scrambling over the rocks,
picking up torn plastic bags and
blue-topped bottles.

Soon the beach is looking better.
Wild and grey, but clean.

The sun peeks out. A sudden splash and flash of silver.
"Look!" Gran cries. "Your seal. He's back."
His head bobs in the pearly-blue water.

"I'm sorry," I say.
He looks at me.
I look at him.
"Things will be different one day," I promise.

My seal splashes. He nods his head.
He dives back down . . .

...into
the wide,
wide sea.